SPIDER'S FIRST DAY AT SCHOOL

BY ROBERT KRAUS

SCHOLASTIC INC.
New York Toronto London Auckland Sydney

FOR PARKER

ISBN 0-590-41091-1

Copyright © 1987 by Robert Kraus.
All rights reserved. Published by Scholastic Inc.

12 11 10 9 8 7 6 5 4 3 2 1   7 8 9/8 0 1 2/9

Printed in the U.S.A.   24
First Scholastic printing, September 1987

Summer was over, and I was feeling sad.

It was the first day of school, and I had the jitters.

Who would my teacher be?
Who would my classmates be?
Spiders don't make friends easily. I was worried.

In the school yard, I said, "Hi," to a bedbug.

"Go away, nasty spider," said the bedbug.

I felt bad.
"Don't feel bad," said a ladybug. "My name is Ladybug, and this is my friend Fly. We'll be your friends."
"Include me out!" said Fly.

Then the school bell rang!
BBBBBBBRRRRRRRRRRRRRIIIIIIIIINNNNNNG!!!

We all hurried to class.
"Good morning, students," said our teacher.
"My name is Miss Quito."
And she certainly was.

Miss Quito taught us our A Bee C's.

Then we learned to count to ten bugs.

We studied art…

and writing.

We studied history…

and bug dancing.

Then the bell rang for recess.

"How do you like school so far?" I asked Ladybug.
"I like it fine," said Ladybug, "but I don't like
recess snack."
"How could you not like recess snack?" I asked.
"Easy," she said. "I forgot to bring mine."
"Me, too," said Fly. "And I'm starving!"

"Don't worry," I said. "Share my snack."
I opened my lunch box, which contained a Swiss
cheese sandwich on rye and some chocolate milk.

"Yummy," said Fly, wolfing down the Swiss cheese sandwich.
"Don't be such a pig, Fly," said Ladybug.
I shared the chocolate milk with Ladybug. It was very tasty.

Then it was time for sports.
"Everybody choose sides for football," said Miss Quito.

We were playing the bedbugs who didn't like me.

They were pretty tough, and we couldn't score a touchdown.

We were pretty tough, too, and they couldn't score a touchdown either.

The score was zero to zero with one minute to play!

We got into a huddle.

"I've got an idea, gang," I said.

"Ideas are cheap," said Fly.

"What is your idea, Spider?" asked Ladybug.

"Let's use the old hidden ball trick," I said.

"But where can we hide the ball?" asked Ladybug.

"You'll see," I said.
Fly hiked the ball to me.
And I hid it in my mouth!

I started running at top speed!
"Where's the ball, where's the ball?"
cried a confused bedbug.
"Fly's got it," said another bedbug.

"No, Ladybug's got it," said another bedbug.
"No, no, Spider's got it," said another bedbug.
You said a mouthful, I thought.

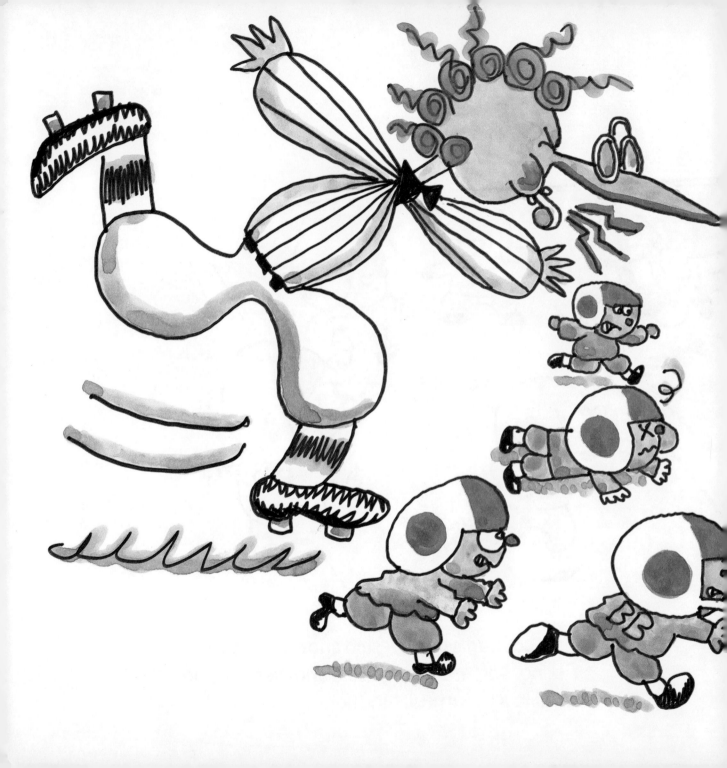

I scored a touchdown!
Miss Quito blew her
whistle!

The game was over!
My team had won!
"You're a star, Spider," said Ladybug.
"Spider, the hero," said Fly.
I was very happy. I was a hero as well
as a spider.

We gave the bedbugs a cheer
for being good losers.
The bedbugs gave us a cheer
for being good winners.
We all felt good.
It was going to be a great
year after all.

The End